About (the) Illustrator

Name: ....

Age: .... Hometown: ....

If I could have one wish come true, it would be:

....

My favorite birthday was: ....

The strangest ice cream flavor I'd create would be:

....

No Birthday Cake for Me

COMPENDIUM®
kids
inspiring possibilities.™

For my birthday this year, instead of cake, I wanted to have an ice cream sundae party.

I imagined lots of ice cream flavors with all my favorite toppings. My parents agreed.

On the morning of my birthday, I thought I heard music playing far down the street.

I opened the front door and saw a parade coming my way.

A brass marching band played music, and people twirled flags.

Acrobats jumped over each other and tumbled in the street.

A group of colorful animals led the parade. I chose my favorite one and climbed up.

We rode off through the town
with the parade behind us.

As we kept going, my neighbors came out of their houses and waved at me.

"Happy birthday!" they called out. "Can we join you?"

I invited them all to come along. My friends chose animals to ride on, too, and trotted beside me to the middle of town.

There was the longest table in the world with ice cream and sauces and candies I had never even seen before.

Everyone gathered around as the brass band played "Happy Birthday to You." 🎵🎶

Then, all the people and animals lined up with bowls and spoons, and I got to go first!

I made a gigantic ice cream sundae with all kinds of delicious things on top.

The scoops stacked all the way up to the sky.

"Thank you all for my birthday celebration!" I said, standing on the back of the tallest animal

so everyone could hear me.
The acrobats threw colorful
confetti and everyone cheered.

I'm already imagining how next year's birthday will be.

WITH SPECIAL THANKS TO THE
ENTIRE COMPENDIUM FAMILY.

CREDITS:

Written by: M.H. Clark
Designed by: Julie Flahiff
Edited by: Amelia Riedler

ISBN: 978-1-935414-96-4

1st printing. Printed in China with soy inks. A0113030017500

COMPENDIUM®
kids
inspiring possibilities.™